MALE OF THE SPECIES

TOM VANDERMOLEN

GRAVESIDE PRESS

For a list of potentially triggering content,
please skip to page 45.

T HEY MET BY A fallen tree in a clearing. He was ten years old. He never knew how old she was.

Martin had spent most of that summer exploring the woods around their new house, but this tree was special. Even partially rotted away, it was the biggest tree he'd ever seen and felt like a relic of some older, wilder forest. It had fallen long ago, created the clearing itself by crushing smaller trees as it crashed to the ground. Its roots had ripped out a crater as big as Martin's bedroom. The fan of decaying roots was taller than Martin and made him think of a dead sea monster washed up on the beach, tentacles torn and rotting.

Fascinated, Martin climbed onto the trunk and approached the bottom. He peered over the clay-caked root stubs. A few experimental kicks sent dirt clods tumbling into the pit.

A cricket, startled from its hiding place, leaped into the pit and landed near a hole in the side of the crater.

There was a blur of motion; the cricket disappeared, replaced by a bundle of white silk. Perched above the bundle was an enormous black spider.

A sound somewhere between a gasp and a sigh escaped Martin's mouth. The spider's body was full and round, the size of a tennis ball, with long and graceful legs. Circling the top of its head were dark, glistening gems that Martin realized were eyes.

It was the most beautiful thing he had ever seen.

The spider filled his mind, made his heart feel trapped behind his ribs, like a bird trying to escape its cage. His hands shook from the need to stroke that black armor, to see if it was as cool and smooth and unyielding as it looked. To cup that ripe abdomen; he knew, absolutely *knew*, it would fit his palm perfectly.

The spider turned and disappeared into the hole.

Martin let out his breath. Then more kicks at the tree roots, until another cricket leaped into the pit. It barely touched the ground before the dark blur was upon it. Another cricket-shaped bundle of silk disappeared down the hole.

This time, though, the spider re-emerged, lingering just inside its den. Watching him.

He fed two more crickets to the spider before it stopped coming back out. Even then he waited for nearly half an hour, tense as a hunting dog on point, before the stiffness in his neck and the darkening sky finally forced him to float home.

He didn't tell his dad about any of it, even as the words threatened to explode out of him and his heart kept transforming into that trapped bird. And the fact that his dad didn't notice how different he was now, how different the world had suddenly become, confirmed he'd done the right thing.

Dinner that night was meatloaf, and Martin ate three helpings.

Martin went back the next day. And the next. By the end of the summer, his butt had worn a smooth patch on the tree trunk.

School started, and he spent the days staring at his teachers, waiting to go home. He began doing his homework sitting on the tree trunk, pausing now and then to peek at the hole or toss in another treat. Being near the spider made him feel smarter. Better.

"Wow," his dad said, looking at Martin's final report card of the year. "Is school here really that much easier than back in...Maryland?" He'd almost said *home*, and Martin knew it.

"Sorta." Then, because Martin still hadn't fully forgiven his dad for moving them to Louisiana: "Also, I've got no friends around here to distract me."

Dad didn't take the bait, but that was alright because Martin had lied a little: he had friends at school now, maybe even more than he'd had back in Maryland. People said things to him, and Martin said similar things back. But it was like having a boring conversation when your favorite song was playing on the radio—he was always really listening to the song. To his real friend.

And as he listened, the years—and the world outside the clearing—spooled past him in a detached blur, like when cartoon characters drove cars, the scenery outside playing in a loop.

Fifth grade was all insects. The supply around the tree didn't last long, so Martin's dad bought him cages of bait crickets from the little store down the road. Martin told him he was fishing at the small pond back in the woods.

By middle school, the spider graduated to mice and guinea pigs. Martin had planned to somehow catch mice at their house, but his dad's hilariously ineffective attempts to get rid of them had apparently, finally, worked. So, Martin took on various odd jobs and became a regular customer of the local pet stores, where he was "that nice boy with the boa constrictors."

Graybow Junior High: ducklings, purchased three at a pop. He almost felt bad about those.

One late summer day, just a few weeks before the start of his junior year of high school, Martin walked through the woods, whistling, a paper bag in one hand and a large canvas sack slung over his other shoulder.

Just shy of the clearing, he stopped whistling and dropped into a crouch, stepping carefully to avoid dry branches and leaves. He padded quietly up the trunk and peered over the mane of roots.

She was waiting, of course. Standing in front of her hole, all eight eyes on him. Her abdomen was now as big as a softball, her head half as large as that. Spread-eagled, her legs could easily reach across a serving platter.

Martin had learned a lot about spiders and knew that a normal spider could not grow to such a size. Even if one somehow did, it would die almost immediately, the loser in a race between asphyxiation and the spider's own crushing weight. Spider physiology was not meant to work at such a scale, just as humans were not built to survive at the scale of elephants.

And yet, here she was. Martin provided for her, and she grew.

"You could at least pretend you didn't know I was coming." He sounded exasperated, but a pleasant warmth tickled his belly.

The spider tapped her two front legs on the ground.

Sitting at his usual place on the trunk, he pulled a writhing bundle of fur from the sack. The kitten, barely two weeks old, meowed pitifully at him, and he used his index finger to gently rub it between the eyes for a moment. Then he tossed it into the pit.

With a cyclone of whirling legs and silk, the spider carried the kitten-shaped bundle back into the hole.

Martin smiled. Girls liked kittens.

He couldn't pin down exactly when he started to think of the spider as female. It could have been her size: female spiders were often larger than male spiders. But really, thinking of the spider as a male made him feel...uncomfortable. Like that whole "queerboy" business.

Martin got along with all of his classmates surprisingly well, given how little he thought about them. The exception: Fred Moran. Ugly, stupid, Fred Moran.

Fred was in Martin's class, and they both worked the same shift as baggers at the Piggly Wiggly. The day before, Martin had been carting out the groceries for one of their regulars, a smiling, gray-haired, grandfatherly type. His name was Mr. Bednarekford, but he told everyone, "Just call me Mr. B!" Martin liked Mr. B; he tipped well.

Martin had loaded the last of the grocery bags into the trunk of Mr. B's car when the old man leaned casually against the rear fender and asked, "So you know where I can get a decent blowjob in this two-bit town?"

Martin, whose only knowledge of blowjobs came from a few porn videos his friend Dave Halber had snuck out of his dad's stash, laughed and said, "No, sir. I guess if I knew that, I wouldn't be standing here right now."

To Martin, Mr. B's comment sounded like the usual locker room stuff at school, and his own response had been pretty solid. But Mr. B's face went splotchy and red, and he slapped an extra-large tip into Martin's hand before driving away. Martin jogged back to the store, pretty proud of his banter game.

Fred Moran was taking his break, sitting in his parents' truck, listening to Hank Williams Jr. and nursing a lip full of snuff. He spat out the truck's window and shouted, "Hey, Hewitt, you earn that tip?"

"You bet!" Martin said, and Fred brayed that obnoxious, high-pitched laugh of his. Mystified, Martin entered the store to more snickering from the other baggers and check-out girls. Finally, one of the girls, Jill McCaffrey, took pity on him and explained that Mr. B had hit on almost all the bag boys at one time or another.

"Guess you were up next," she said, shrugging. Then she saw Martin's expression. "Aw, It's okay. Old guys make passes at me all the time. You get used to it."

At the end of the shift, though, Fred Moran walked past him and said, "Hey, queerboy, want me to drop you off at Mr. B's house on my way home?"

A sudden roaring in Martin's ears drowned out the laughter of the others, and only one thing kept him from ripping that ridiculous hyena laugh right out of Fred's disgusting hole: an image of Fred, his head encircled by slender black limbs, fangs plunging in and out of his neck, the laugh replaced by a high-pitched scream.

He became aware of Jill's hand on his shoulder. "Don't mind Fred," she said, rolling her eyes. "He's just jealous because Mr. B never hits on *him*."

But Martin did mind. And now, watching the spider emerge from her hole, he wondered how deep that hole was. If there was, say, a Fred-sized opening among all those desiccated bodies.

"You'd like that, wouldn't you?" he asked her softly.

She stared at him.

He dug out another kitten, under handing it into the depression.

Dark blur. Whirling legs. Neatly wrapped bundle.

Down the hole.

Martin almost pulled a hard-boiled egg from the paper bag, then winced and grabbed an apple instead, hoping she hadn't seen it.

In all the years he'd known her, the spider had never laid eggs. Not that he was around her 24/7 or anything; in fact, during the worst of winter, she disappeared entirely into what he assumed was a state of hibernation. But he never saw egg sacs or little ones.

Recently, he'd realized the topic made her uncomfortable, so Martin respected her privacy and avoided the topic. But the reasons were obvious: she was truly unique in this world. That meant no males of her species either, so no mating, no babies. It meant being alone, only connecting with others in a very particular, lethal way.

Martin had begun to understand he'd never have kids, either.

How could he, in a world filled with Fred Morans? People who hated uniqueness, who wanted to crush it, to mock it from the safety of their boring little lives. Being unique was hard.

He saw her looking at him and his mood lightened.

"At least we're unique together, right?" He smiled at her agreement and bit into the apple.

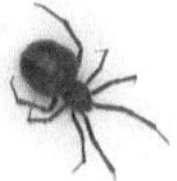

By his senior year, Martin could walk to the clearing with his eyes closed. Today he was trying to do exactly that, squinting against the tiny blades of sunlight that cut through the treetops and into his brain. He squeezed his eyes against the throbbing in his head, and an image immediately flashed across the darkness: a jumbled collage of dark sheets, long tanned limbs, streaked-blonde hair, and shockingly pale breasts. His eyes popped open, and this time he welcomed the pain. *You deserve it, you idiot.*

First mistake: going to one of Dave Halber's increasingly infamous house parties.

Second mistake: losing track of his alcohol intake at the party. Halber's parents were like Bigfoot—legendary but rarely seen—and Dave had become an excellent and persuasive host-slash-bartender.

Third mistake: getting isolated from the crowd with Jill McCaffrey, who, according to Dave, at least, had the hots for Martin.

And after that, the mistakes came too fast to count.

Before he even realized he was drunk, they were in the Halber guest bedroom, Jill's mouth was all over him, and she'd already removed both of their shirts. Martin, too panicked to speak, was on the verge of punching his way out when Jill abruptly pulled her lips away from his neck, laughed, wiped her face with his shirt, and passed out.

Shaking, Martin sat on the edge of the bed, exhausted from relief and alcohol. He rubbed his face viciously with his palms, then turned and evaluated the situation.

Jill was motionless, miniskirt hiked up to her waist, snoring slightly. He turned her more on her side, so she wouldn't puke and choke to death.

Deep breath. What story would work here? Jill probably wouldn't remember much past the kissing, and everyone saw her pawing him as they entered the guest room. So...some second base-third base stuff happened, then Jill passed out. Martin, the trustworthy but otherwise totally normal heterosexual male, is frustrated but understanding. Her friends take her home. The word "queerboy" never occurs to anyone.

And Martin never, ever, goes to another Dave Halber party.

He nodded and looked around the room, trying to see it with a party forensics eye. He untangled her bra from one of the pillows and tossed it onto the floor. Then he picked it up and draped it over a bedpost. The miniskirt was fine as it was, hiked up to her waist. The question was about her panties. She had started shimmying out of them, and now they were down past her ass in the back, not quite covering her pubic hair in the front. That was good, but was it enough? Should he leave them on her, or take them? Sometimes girls left them behind, didn't they? Or was that a movie thing?

He pulled her panties down to her mid-thigh, examined the effect. Crept to the door and looked from there. Crept back and pulled the miniskirt's hem down a few inches, just enough to cover her private areas; some guy may come in before Jill's friends could cover her up, after all.

He nodded again. This could actually work. His reputation might even improve.

Five minutes, then leave. He sat on the bed, hating the feeling of being drunk, his senses and thoughts blunted and slow. He watched Jill, listening to her breathing for signs of congestion or retching.

He'd been staring at her for a full minute before he suddenly *got* how attractive Jill was. He had known this for a while, of course, but more as an academic fact. It was one of the reasons she was first on his list of girlfriend candidates; she hit most of the items on Martin's checklist: long blonde hair, a very symmetrical face, almost no acne, athletic body, popular without being obsessed with popularity. She wore yellow a lot, and Martin liked yellow. She was nice and easy to talk to. Guys talked about her a lot. Best of all, she had a "good girl" reputation, so would be unlikely to pressure him into sex. *Better uncheck that box now,* he thought, grimacing.

But it occurred to him now that maybe the checklist didn't really do her justice. That gymnastics-toned body, the long blonde hair and smooth skin. Now that he was really looking at her, he could see that she was...exciting. A feeling of discovery, of teetering on the edge of something unknown but thrilling, rose up within him.

Her bra and panties were matching black satin, with some lace trim. They had a soft, dark sheen in the dim light. He liked how black they were, how shiny. Like dark armor.

And he suddenly realized he had an erection.

It was not his first, of course; like most normal boys, Martin often woke up with an erection. He knew other young men were weirdly obsessed with theirs, but to Martin his erections were pointless biological oddities, like an appendix.

But now, something about the sight of Jill's panties, that glorious intersection of smooth, tanned skin and shiny darkness, made his entire body tremble in a fascinating new way.

In a blur of fumbling and zippers, his cock was suddenly

in his hand. He was quietly masturbating, eyes locked on Jill's blissfully unaware form.

He was vaguely aware that this was the best thing he'd ever felt. It was fucking *amazing*, in fact. Air whistled in his nose as his breathing quickened.

Then he tilted his head to get a better view, and the light shifted on the dark satin. Suddenly he imagined *her* on the other side of Jill's body. Advancing with that sensuous, slow, utterly confident pace. He trembled so much his teeth began to chatter. His strokes grew faster, almost painful. He watched the fantasy spider toy with Jill, exploring her body with long, lovely legs. Then, just as he felt himself about to come, she plunged her fangs into Jill's neck, and now they were both pumping their fluids into Jill's body. His real-world orgasm was so intense that he cried out involuntarily—screamed, in fact—and slumped weakly onto the bed.

As abruptly as it'd seized him, the lust abandoned him, leaving a cold cavity filled with shame. The sudden change was more dizzying and disorienting than being drunk. What had seemed so powerful, so right just seconds before—well, not *right*, exactly, but deliciously, powerfully, *wrong*—now seemed pathetic and small.

Jill murmured slightly in her sleep. Martin froze, shaking from tension, until her breathing deepened again.

Eyes wide, he stuffed his withered, traitor penis back into his pants. He took deep breaths, but still the panic kept bubbling up. Jesus, what if someone came in now? Jill passed out, about a gallon of jizz all over the room—

He grabbed some Kleenex from the bedside table and began mopping up his mess as best he could. The Kleenex just seemed to smear his semen around, then shredded into tiny bits all over Mrs. Halber's comforter.

Fuck it, good enough. He had to go, he had to get the fuck out of this house and away from Jill and this mess he'd made in this room. He needed some time and space to think. Let Dave explain the stains to his parents, and fuck him anyway for getting Martin into this.

He fumbled the door open and stepped into the party, the sudden blast of light and noise battering his thoughts into an overheated slurry. People turned to look at him.

Martin froze. They wanted details; people always wanted details. Always wanted you to prove you were just like them.

He couldn't just say, "Third base, man, it was awesome!" Had Jill given him a blowjob or a hand job? Was one better than the other? What if Jill didn't like giving blowjobs, would her friends get suspicious? And which one would make him scream like that? And why did he have to scream, Jesus, they probably thought Jill had murdered him—

"There he is!" Dave Halber hooted, drink in hand, the other held out in a high-five. "There's my main—"

"It was both!" Martin shrieked.

He woke at two in the afternoon, his head one giant, throbbing blood vessel. Craving fresh air, he stumbled into his clothes and went outside. His feet took him to the tree on their own.

She probably won't even come out, he thought, lip curling into a self-pitying snarl. She had been weirdly standoffish the last couple of weeks, sometimes barely emerging from her hole at all. Like it was too much effort.

Or you're too much effort.

He told himself she was just older and slower—they'd been together for seven years, after all.

Or maybe she's bored. Of you.

The thought made his skin flame but his gut cold.

He climbed onto the tree trunk and stomped his feet deliberately on his way to his usual seat by the roots. Each stomp sent a hot flare of pain through his skull, but it was worth it, because maybe it would wake her ass up, get her to notice something besides her own—

She was outside her hole, waiting for him.

Martin flinched in surprise, then flinched again from the jolt to his head. He grunted, rubbing his temples, and glared at her.

Now the size of a small dog, her abdomen as large as a basketball, the spider was a cool black sculpture of sleek, lethal lines. Despite the pain and doubt that filled his head, her gravity pulled at him as strongly as ever.

So annoying.

"No, I didn't bring you anything. Sorry to disappoint you, Your Majesty."

The spider stared.

"How can you be hungry? I just gave you a fucking dog yesterday. Or day before yesterday." He shook his head slowly. "You know, there are only so many 'free puppy' ads out there, and it's not like I can go back for seconds." He blurted humorless laughter. "Jesus, last week some woman at Wal-Mart asked me how the puppy she gave me was doing. Lucky my dad wasn't with me."

The light glinted off her black eyes.

"No, that gray mutt, from a few weeks back. I think. I guess they're all gray to you. And no, I didn't tell her, I'm not an idiot." He closed his eyes, and his mind showed him a quick flash of Jill's legs again. "I'm just saying that my part isn't easy either, okay?"

Her right front leg tapped the ground, twice.

Martin swallowed the sudden lump in his throat. "I'm sorry, too." He sighed, then sat: a kind of controlled collapse onto the trunk. He scrubbed his face with his hands. Still not meeting her gaze, he asked, "Is this—are we okay? I mean, you'd tell me, wouldn't you? If you were…I don't know." Shrugged. "Bored? With us?"

Her middle-left leg lifted, slowly lowered.

"No, of course *I'm* not." Face flushed, he dropped his gaze again, suddenly sure she already knew everything. "It's just…we used to be a team, you know? But lately, you seem kind of…" *Bitchy.* "…off."

She stared.

A flare of anger burned in his gut. "See, here we go," he said. "When I try to talk about real stuff, about us, you shut down."

The spider's rear left leg tapped the sandy ground.

"How have I *not* shown commitment?" he said, forcing his suddenly clumsy lips to form the words. "And what exactly is wrong with dogs and cats? I never saw you turn one down."

A single tap.

"Seriously?" Martin's nostrils flared and he nodded, mouth drawn tight. "Okay. How about this? How about

I bring a *person* next time?"

A pause. Then the spider's front left leg raised just a bit, slowly lowered again.

"Well, I was thinking maybe..." A clammy sweat broke out on his body. "A girl."

It was a strange thing to have those words leave his lips. He could almost see them, slowly expanding like balloons, filling the space between him and the spider.

Her eyes were eight black lasers, beaming hot judgment into his face. Martin swallowed down another wave of nausea, then opened his mouth to laugh and tell her he was just joking, just kidding around. And hey, who else wants a dog around here besides me? But he stopped when he saw her move.

Slowly, her left rear leg rose into the air, followed by one of her middle right legs.

"Of course I meant it," he stammered, pulse banging a drum in his temples.

Her legs dropped to the ground again, then a single left front tap.

"I don't know. I have to figure out the who before I know the when, right?" His mouth felt dry and slimy at the same time. He wiped his lips.

One tap, right front leg.

"No, not Jill. That'd be stupid." *Especially after last*

night. "But there are plenty of other girls, ones I don't know as well. Maybe even one of the strippers up in Alverton—"

Both front legs, one tap each.

Martin blinked. "Well, of course it'd be a girl, why—"

Right front leg, two quick taps.

"Because I'm not a queerboy!" Martin said, a little louder than he'd intended.

She stared.

"I think I've proven my commitment already," he said stiffly. "You get to do your thing, so I'd like to do mine, too. It's...biology. And it's only fair."

Left rear leg, slowly raised.

They stared at each other.

"Fine." Martin's hands went to his hips, his mouth a tense line. "But next time *I* get to choose. That's what being a team means, you know."

Another tap.

Martin nodded, trembling a little now, face slightly pale.

But his heart was that little bird again, fluttering in his chest.

"Fred's out. Visiting grandparents in Corpus Christi." Mr. Houseley, the Piggly Wiggly manager, furrowed his bushy eyebrows. "Why, did you need to switch your shifts?"

Struggling to keep his expression blank, Martin shook his head slightly and mumbled something. Then he went to the store's claustrophobic restroom, checked the stalls were empty, and screamed without opening his mouth until snot boiled out of his nostrils.

Then he took a deep, slightly shaky breath, checked his face in the mirror, and made adjustments until he looked reasonably normal again.

He would have to make do. Maybe get a goat or something to tide her over until Fred got back from his—

The restroom door swung open. Martin turned and froze.

"Oh!" Mr. B said, eyes wide. "Martin! Are you, uh, on your way out?"

Martin smiled.

"I'll be damned," Mr. B panted, peering at Martin's tree. A bead of sweat dripped from his nose. The bald spot on the crown of his head was a bright, unhappy red;

Martin half-expected to see heat waves shimmering off of it. "I thought you were making a joke. You know, like 'big wood.'" He did air quotes with his fingers and guffawed. When Mr. B laughed, his tongue stuck slightly out of his mouth. It made Martin queasy.

But Martin returned the laugh, still relieved they'd finally reached the clearing. There was a good mile of forest between here and where they'd left Mr. B's car at Graybow's tiny civil airstrip, and Martin had been afraid he'd either get them lost in the woods or Mr. B would die of a heart-attack on the way. But it'd been easy, as if bringing Mr. B here was preordained. Inevitable.

"So what do you think?" Martin gestured at the pit, using the movement to disguise a quick glance at the spider hole. She was hiding.

"Hold on, this is it?" Mr. B cocked an eyebrow. "Your 'secret place' is a hole in the ground?"

"It's nice." Martin slid down the dirt sides of the pit and suppressed a shiver; being in her space made his skin tingle and his cock twitch. "Come on down!"

Mr. B peered down into the pit, nose wrinkled. Martin could clearly see the jungles of gray hairs in his nostrils. "It's *dirt*, Martin."

Does he want me or not? "I thought you wanted dirty." He tried to strike a seductive pose, but ended up just standing awkwardly, hand on one hip.

"Right now, I just want a shower." Mr. B flapped his shirt a few times and Martin caught the odor of old-man sweat. "Maybe we both need one." A lecherous smile.

Martin's own smile felt like a squirming, living thing that was trying to escape his face. "We can do both. You know, dirty, then clean."

Mr. B took a step back and pointed in the direction they'd come. "I've got a bottle of bourbon in the car, we can—"

Fuck it. Martin unbuttoned his shorts and pulled them down. His erection bobbed in the open air.

Mr. B stared. "Well," he said, breathless.

Martin kept the smile going, eyes on Mr. B but straining to detect any movement from the spider hole.

Dirt cascaded down the sides of the pit as Mr. B picked his way down. Martin took a careful step back, keeping the spider hole between them. She had to be watching.

Mr. B moved toward him. "That for me?" he asked, slurring as if his lips had gone to sleep. He was lined up perfectly in front of the hole.

Now, Martin thought.

Mr. B took another step forward. His mouth was open, tongue visible.

Martin realized he was backed up against the side of the

pit, which suddenly seemed very small. *What the fuck is she waiting for?* "Come on, do it!"

A smile split Mr. B's red face. "What do you want first?"

Now Martin could see Mr. B's erection, could almost feel its moist heat radiating at him.

"*What are you waiting for?*" Martin screamed.

Mr. B took a step back, eyes wide. "Take it easy, no need to rush, we—" Then his eyes narrowed. He backed away, craning his neck to scan the trees. "Look," he said loudly, "I don't want nothing to do with your little homo plans, Martin."

For one spinning, dumbfounded moment, Martin thought Mr. B was talking to the spider. Then Mr. B looked back at Martin, his soft grandfather's face now hard and angry. "Where are your friends, huh? Where's your buddy Fred?"

Shock rattled through Martin's body. "He's not my friend," he said, voice barely above a whisper.

"I guess he isn't," Mr. B snorted. "Looks like your buddies bugged out on your little queer-bashing party."

"My—my what?" Martin grunted and tried to pull his pants up, but found he barely had the strength to stand. He covered himself with his hands. *Where was she?* Mr. B's red face blurred as tears formed in Martin's eyes.

"Fucking pansy." Mr. B shook his head. "We'll see what

the cops think about you trying to mug me."

"Cops?" Martin wailed, disgusted by the weakness in his own voice.

Mr. B climbed out of the pit, chicken legs pumping. "Damn straight." He leaned against the tree trunk, removed one shoe, shook dirt from it, put it back on. "Of course," he smiled, "if you can get your 'little wood' there to come out again, maybe we can talk. Maybe I'll let you—"

From the top of the tree trunk, a shadow leaped onto Mr. B's shoulders.

Mr. B yelped, staggering forward under her weight, then yelped again when her fangs plunged into his neck. He whirled and twisted, cursing, trying to grab his attacker, but the spider avoided him easily, dancing around on his shoulders. Mr. B took a few blind stumbling steps before toppling into the pit. The spider rode him down like a rodeo champion, staying on top of the old man until he rolled into Martin's feet.

The impact finally broke Martin's paralysis. He held down Mr. B's legs while she worked his upper body, her fangs striking again and again, pumping Mr. B with her venom.

And then it happened: her leg brushed against Martin's arm.

For one brief, eternal, electric moment, all of Martin's senses were focused on that touch. Her soft hairs, tickling his skin. Her armor, smooth but unyielding. Most of all, the undeniable reality of *her*. His erection returned so fast he thought it would split like a hot dog in the microwave.

Demurely, she pretended not to notice.

By the time Martin could think again, only Mr. B's eyes were still moving, rolling in their sockets like those of a maddened horse. Martin smiled into those eyes. "*We* did this to you," he said. "I want you to know that." Then he rolled Mr. B into the hole.

Only then did Martin finally fall to his knees, masturbating. He came almost instantly, jetting long streamers of semen onto the pine needles and dirt of the pit floor.

It was true, what people said: the first time was magical.

It took a week before Mr. B's empty car finally raised any suspicions, another week before the *Graybow Observer* printed a box on page three asking for anyone with information on his disappearance to contact the Sheriff's office. No one had missed him; a single sentence mentioned Mr. B was a widower, estranged from his children.

Then nothing. No more articles in the paper. No police sweeps. No one even remarked on his absence at Piggly Wiggly. It was as if Mr. B, with his red face and interest in bag boys, had never existed. To be safe, Martin stayed away from the clearing for three full weeks, sometimes trembling with the need to see her again. The sights and sounds of Mr. B's death passed through his waking moments in an endless loop.

Finally, late one Saturday afternoon while his dad was playing golf, Martin walked up the path, bringing two guinea pigs he'd bought from the pet store up in Alverton. Just a little something to celebrate.

That bird in his chest fluttered pleasantly as he neared the clearing. And he smiled because she was waiting for him, as usual.

But something felt different.

He cocked his head. "Something wrong?"

She didn't answer.

"I know, I'm sorry I waited so long to visit again." Martin smiled again and held up the bag. "But I brought you a little present to—"

Something small and quick scampered out. It was all legs and energy, a brown and black blur zipping back and forth along the lip of the hole.

A little spider.

"Who the fuck is that?" Martin whispered.

She ignored him, her attention focused on the little one.

He fumbled in his pocket for his keychain penlight. The dim circle it projected was just bright enough to reveal the huddled forms inside the hole.

There was a Mr. B-shaped object in the hole, still partly wrapped in silk. But now he was covered with hundreds of tiny spiders, crawling busily over his body, boiling from his mouth in a bristling stream.

Martin stared. A part of him—the smallest part—was fascinated: *so she* does *lay eggs.*

And then: *don't eggs need to be fertilized?*

His face burned. "When? When did you—" He wiped tears away savagely and glared at her. "*When?!*"

She didn't even have the decency to look embarrassed.

"Oh, am I not *male* enough for you? Is that it?" Martin made a noise that was half-laugh, half-wail. "Did you at least eat him afterwards?"

She turned her back to him, facing the hole and her children. Her little bastards.

"Hey! Look at me!"

Still, she ignored him, as if he were speaking a foreign language.

He picked up the sack of guinea pigs. He wanted to say something cutting, something that would hurt in the most meaningful way possible. Something he could remember later and feel good about. What he managed was: "Fucking present, *bitch*!" Then he threw the sack into the hole.

The sack—which also held a can of soda for himself—struck the mass of Mr. B and baby spiders dead center, crushing some of the babies. Martin saw one wobble away with a missing leg. The rest scattered in panic.

"Fucking ignore me now, you—" He turned to her and saw that, maybe for the first time ever, he had her complete attention.

It was the most terrifying thing he'd ever seen.

"Wait." The word leaked out in a moistureless sigh, barely audible even to himself.

Martin turned and ran.

He'd never run like this in his life. He did not look back. He was barely able to breathe. But after an eternity of bracing for the impact of fangs and legs on his back, he finally slammed against his back door, adrenaline-clumsy hands pawing at the doorknob.

Locked.

By the time it occurred to him that the keys were in his pocket, he had already twisted to face her, ready to plead, to beg.

The porch and the yard were empty.

He collapsed onto the faded wood planks of the porch.

Martin jerked awake in the darkness of his bedroom.

"Oh, Jesus," he whispered. He had somehow twisted his covers into a cocoon around his body; both were soaked in sweat. The nightmare was already fading from his mind, but his insides, still tense and trembling, remembered it clearly. He had to piss like crazy.

Tap-tap-tap.

A dry clicking, like nails on glass, came from the window over his bed, just out of his peripheral vision.

On the far wall, a shadow, cast by something with a bulbous body and long legs, moved in the moonlight projecting through the window. Something one pane of glass and two feet away from his head.

Tap-tap.

Martin froze, not even able to tremble.

Just before dawn, he silently released his bladder, tears running down his cheeks. Sometime after that, the shadow dropped away, and the tapping stopped.

But still he didn't move, not until dawn came an eternity later.

The hickory tree's bark was rough but comforting against Martin's back. Without looking, he eased the heavy can of gasoline to the ground and put both hands on the shotgun. Checked the shotgun to make sure it hadn't somehow unloaded itself in the five minutes since he'd last checked it.

The sky was swirling and steely, a late spring storm on its way. No rain yet, but curdled sheets of gray clouds obscured the sun. A near-constant wind sent the trees and bushes swaying and plucked at his hair.

Where was she? It had taken him an hour to leave his house, checking the front and back porches, poking the gun into the crawl space and the eaves and every corner. Afraid of an ambush, he'd avoided trails on his way here, stepping on layers of pine needles to soften his footsteps, and entering the clearing from behind the hickory tree, the opposite of his usual approach.

She couldn't be expecting that, right?

Martin raised the shotgun to his shoulder, feeding off

the trickle of confidence it gave him. *Bitch knows where I live*, he thought, sighting down the barrel. *But she doesn't know what a shotgun—*

His eyes widened as the implication finally hit. *How long has she known where I live?*

The mice that had plagued their house until…the winter after he'd met her. The same winter he'd spent days staring at the hole, wondering if she was sleeping in the darkness there.

Apparently not.

Shuddering, he put both hands back on the gun, wishing it were a twelve-gauge pump-action model, instead of his father's barely used, over-and-under twenty-eight-gauge skeet gun.

Do it methodically, like she would.

With his cheek against the cool reassurance of the gunstock, he focused down the barrel, searching the underbrush. Nothing.

Easing forward, he checked the top of the tree trunk. Nothing.

More quiet steps, pulse thudding rapidly against his eardrums. The hole came into view over the trembling front sight.

Nothing.

At the edge of the pit, he flicked the switch on the

flashlight he'd taped to the shotgun's barrel and shone it into the hole.

Nothing but baby spiders and dried-out husks.

Martin's breath grew short. Where was she? She could be hiding anywhere, she could still be at his house, somewhere he hadn't checked. And how could he ever be sure anywhere was safe if—?

Stop it! He stumbled back to the relative safety of the hickory, letting the tree protect his rear while he tried to breathe.

The sun poked through the clouds, casting shadows of hickory branches and a large gourd across the clearing. The sudden movement made him jump. *Jesus, you idiot, don't let her psyche you out, she's got a brain the size of a—*

His skin and gut went suddenly cold. *A gourd—?*

Martin whirled, fumbling the shotgun up, just as she leapt from her perch in the hickory tree branches.

As Martin lurched backward, his feet tangled, and he felt himself fall. Just as his back slammed onto the sandy earth, his fingers spasmed on the trigger.

A sudden, violent slap of sound by his ear. The spray of shotgun pellets ripped the spider in half, shredding her thorax, her full, enticing abdomen bursting like an obscene water balloon.

And then, somehow, Martin was left alive, staring at the

boiling sky, ears ringing, nostrils filled with a sharp odor like vinegar.

He burned the babies.

Some tried to run after he started pouring the gas into the hole, but he crushed them under his shoes as they emerged, the soles sliding as the treads filled with innards. The rest died instantly, curling into tortured balls as the flames filled the hole. The webbing that shrouded Mr. B dissolved in the fire like cotton candy in water. Behind him were countless smaller bundles of webbing and bone.

Then, bit by bit, he fed her to the fire as well.

He sagged to his knees in front of the hole, his mind a buzzing blankness. A thought pierced the deadness: *where's the Male's body?*

She must have eaten him. But none of the corpses in the hole looked the right size.

What if there wasn't one?

Martin's brow furrowed. Babies came from eggs, eggs had to be fertilized by sperm, which—

And suddenly he remembered the last time he'd been on his knees in this pit, ejaculating for what seemed like an eternity.

He shook his head slowly. Biologically, it was impossible.

But *she* had been impossible, too.

He looked at the little curled bodies with widening eyes. His mouth opened to scream, but all that escaped his throat was a low, feeble whimper, full of bile and guilt and the aching recognition of a life that could have been.

Martin did the things damned people did. He dated. Went to college, finished college, got a job. Embraced every tepid moment of this gray life. Watched helplessly as those moments accumulated into years.

Things improved somewhat after he moved away from Graybow, from the scene of his crime. Entire days might go by without him thinking of her.

But at night he dreamed of a dark, slender limb brushing his skin.

Jill was talking.

"Mmm?" His gaze was locked, unseeing, on the trees outside.

"Why didn't your dad ever remarry?"

Martin turned. His movements felt slow and muffled, like everything since the funeral.

Jill was crouched in front of one of the boxes from the attic, hair tied back in a ponytail, clothes dusty from cleaning. She held up a framed photograph.

"Oh." Martin nodded. "He always said he never found anyone who could hold a candle to my mom."

She looked at the wedding portrait with a wistful expression. "She must have been an amazing woman."

"Honestly, I don't really remember her." Martin shrugged, his mind still outside. "Maybe it's just that Hewitt men never forget their first loves."

Jill smiled. "Aw, so sweet."

He almost asked what she was talking about, then caught himself. He knelt beside her and gave her a quick kiss, then pulled open a box from the pile in the living room. "Jesus, I didn't realize how much of a packrat my dad became while I was gone—" he stopped and took a deep breath when he saw the box was filled with Star Wars action figures. The ones he'd played with that first summer in Graybow.

His throat closed up and he wiped his eyes. Jill put her arms around him and kissed his forehead.

The baby started to cry, that whiny I-want-attention sound that made Martin's ears hurt.

"I've got her," he said. "I kind of need to get away from this for a minute."

She nodded. "Of course, sweetie. I'll plow through this. Why don't you take her for a walk, get some fresh air?"

It was a fine fall day, the kind he loved the most, if a bit chilly. Humming snatches of songs into his daughter's tiny ear, he made a few perfunctory laps of the backyard. It was rougher than he remembered; Dad had lost interest in yardwork as the cancer progressed. The entrance to the trail was almost completely overgrown, but somehow Martin found himself walking along it, moving on rails through the undergrowth. He sang the same song over and over, holding his daughter close, like a shield, his mind carefully blank.

Absurdly, he was amazed the clearing was still there, that the tree and the hole hadn't ceased to exist, like the dream they must have been. Yet he was also surprised anything had changed at all, as if the clearing should have been frozen in place, waiting for his return.

But all that had happened was time. The massive trunk was now a mound of rot. New bushes and saplings grew in open defiance. Time had simply continued, dragging them all along for the ride.

"Not all of us," he whispered into his daughter's hair, and the smooth curve of her skull suddenly felt like a shotgun stock against his cheek. Tears blurred his vision.

When he wiped the tears away, he saw her, waiting for him in the pit.

No. This couldn't be her. This spider was too small, barely a foot across. And her legs were banded with brown striping.

Camouflage. With that brown striping, she must have blended into the weeds around the hole, hiding while Martin killed her siblings and his reason for living. His mistake had given this brave little survivor a second chance at life.

And now...she could be *his* second chance at life.

He was ready now. He'd been through so much these long gray years. He had the strength now to prove his commitment. To be the Male he always should have been.

He walked forward, legs shaking. The thing in his hands was struggling, making noises.

When he got closer to his daughter, Martin saw that she had her mother's eyes.

Tom Vandermolen started out life as a military brat, born in Japan to a US Navy sailor and a Japanese mother, but raised primarily in the American South. A childhood of books, comics, movies, excellent English grades, and mediocre math grades resulted in a collection of short-story rejections and, inexplicably, a physics degree. After college, what should have been a short enlistment as a nuclear submarine officer somehow became a twenty-two-year career as a Navy intelligence officer. No one is sure how any of this happened.

Now retired from the military and working as a data scientist, Tom lives in Seattle with his wife, Yvette, who is always his first reader (and editor).

tomvandermolen.com

animal death

homophobia (use of mild slurs)

staging of an unconscious inebriated woman's body

sexual content

sexual content involving a non-human

suggested infanticide (off-page)

*Thank you for supporting Graveside Press and our authors.
One of the biggest ways you can help is to leave a star rating
or a review wherever you purchased your copy!*

STAY SPOOKY.

Wanna come hang out with the ghouls?
gravesidepress.carrd.co

Stay up to date with Graveside news and exclusive stories.
graveside-press.com